KT-399-941

BAINTE DEN STOC

WITHDRAWN FROM DLR LIBRARIES STOCK

Ideas Box!

BAINTE DEN STOC

WITHDRAWN FROM DLR LIBRARIES STOCK

Where You Live

BAINTE DEN STOC

WITHDRAWN FROM DLR LIBRARIES STOCK

I bet you get a good view of the local area from there!

Jillian Powell

W
FRANKLIN WATTS
LONDON • SYDNEY

espresso
education

First published in 2011

Franklin Watts
338 Euston Road
London NW1 3BH

Franklin Watts Australia
Level 17/207 Kent Street
Sydney, NSW 2000

Text and illustration © Franklin Watts 2011

The Espresso characters are originated
and designed by Claire Underwood and
Pesky Ltd.

The Espresso characters are the property of
Espresso Education Ltd.

All rights reserved.

A CIP catalogue record for this book is
available from the British Library.

ISBN: 978 1 4451 0395 2
Dewey number: 307.3

Series Editor: Sarah Peutrill
Art Director: Jonathan Hair
Series Designer: Matthew Lilly
Illustrations by Artful Doodlers Ltd.

Printed in China

Franklin Watts is a division of
Hachette Children's Books,
an Hachette UK company
www.hachette.co.uk

Picture credits: Mark Burrow,
Nottinghamshire, UK/Shutterstock:
29t. Bryan Busovicki/Shutterstock:
29c. James Chetwode/Alamy: 12br.
Chris Banwell-Clode/istockphoto: 7b.
Jim O'Donnell/Alamy: 25cl. Greg
Balfour Evans/Alamy: 17tr. Francis
Frith Collection: 17tl. Jen Frooms/
Shutterstock: 5br. Chris Leachman/
Shutterstock: 1, 12bl. Richard
Majlinder/Shutterstock: 6t. Nigel Paul
Monkton/Shutterstock: 3, 26b.
Photogenes: 16b Pixel Memoirs/
Shutterstock: 29b. Purple Marbles/
Alamy: 13c. Helene Rogers/
arkreligion.com: 18cl. Edward Shaw/
istockphoto: 19tr. Shout/Alamy: 24b.
Jens Stolt/Shutterstock: 9c. Lori
Walter/istockphoto: 7t. witchcraft/
Shutterstock: 5bl. J van der Wolf/
Shutterstock: 8c. Adam Woolfitt/
Corbis: 5t. Every attempt has been
made to clear copyright. Should there
be any inadvertent omission please
apply to the publisher for rectification.

Contents

The Espresso friends:

I'm Sal and I'm 10.

I'm Ash and I'm 8.

I'm Scully and I'm Ash's dog.

I'm Kim and I'm 7.

I'm Polly and I'm 6.

I'm Scrap and I live with Polly and Eddy.

I'm Polly's brother, Eddy, and I'm 3.

Pages with this symbol have a downloadable photocopiable sheet (see page 30).

What is special about where you live?

Ash and Kim are on a treasure hunt in their local area. They have to find different buildings and features from clues and tick them off on a chart. The first person to fill in the chart wins tickets to the local football match. But Ash and Kim are still looking for the door knocker!

Treasure Hunt

What?	Where?	Map ref.	
A weathervane	Florence Road	C2	✓
A railway bridge	Station Road	C5	✓
A chapel	Church Road	E1	✓
A house with a blue plaque	Mayfield Avenue	B3	✓
A house with a green front door	High Street	E3	✓
A house with a lion door knocker	Mayfield Avenue	A4	

Blue plaques mark houses which have famous connections because someone important was born or lived there. They were first used in London in 1866 and are now used all around the world.

LONDON COUNTY COUNCIL
SAMUEL L. CLEMENS
"MARK TWAIN"
1835 – 1910
American Writer
lived here in
1896–7

Ash and Kim are using a street map which has a grid of squares. They plot the map grid reference by finding the place they are looking for and reading which square it falls into by alphabetical letter and number.

Geography spot: your own treasure hunt

Can you find any of the features on Ash and Kim's list in your local area? What buildings and features could you include if you were organising a treasure hunt?

Finding out about the past

Ash's class has been doing a history project about their local area. They have learned to be history detectives by looking for clues that can tell us the age of a building.

Ash has used a checklist to study one of the oldest houses in the area.

Fast facts: old or new?

Old Materials
- stone
- brick
- timber
- lime plaster and mortar

Old Windows
- Small – casements or sash

Old Storeys
- One to three

Old Chimneys
- One or more chimney stacks

New Materials
- concrete
- brick
- PVC
- steel
- glass

New Windows
- Large – 'picture' windows

New Storeys
- Can have multi-storeys

New Chimneys
- No chimney stacks

Where is the building?
No 4 Hay Hill, off the market place.

How many storeys does it have?
Three.

What building materials have been used?
Brick, lime and timber.

Windows: what shape/size are they?
Small rectangular windows.

Does the building have any of these features?
Timber frame or beams Yes.
Chimney stacks Yes.
Date carved over a porch or doorway No.
Crooked windows or walls Yes.

History spot: looking for clues

Some new buildings are made to look old. This house has been built in a traditional style to look like an old house, but there are clues to its age. Can you suggest what they are?

Quiz:
What were windows made of before glass was invented?

A) Bone

B) Animal skin

C) Horn

Quiz answers are on page 32.

Schools can also be old buildings. Some were built during Victorian times (1837–1901) and are still used today. Other schools were built more recently, or are almost new.

In Victorian times girls and boys entered some schools through separate entrances. You can still see signs like this today.

GIRLS

What is the natural history of your area?

Kim and Polly have been on a farm open day. The farm in their local area is a mixed farm, which means the farmer grows crops and also keeps animals including cows for milking.

In their local area, there is plenty of grass pasture for the cattle to graze and lots of rain to keep the grass and crops growing.

These dairy cows graze outdoors in the summer months.

The soil in their local area is clay. In other areas, it can be sandy or chalky. Soil can also be acid or alkaline. It is important for farmers and gardeners to know about their soil as some plants grow better in one type of soil rather than another.

Kim and Polly do a soil test on the farm. They collect samples of soil in clean glass jars and mix in some water. They add a tablespoon of vinegar to one sample and a tablespoon of baking powder to the other. If the vinegar fizzes the soil is alkaline, but if the baking powder fizzes it is acid. They find out that clay soil is alkaline.

On the farm there are several types of habitat that support different types of plants and animals. Kim makes a list of some that they see:

Farm habitat list

Hedgerow
blackbird
wren
hawthorn
blackthorn
Woodland
squirrel
beetle
oak
beech

Meadow
buttercup
grasses
orange tip butterfly
Pond
ducks
frogspawn
water mint
rushes

This orange tip butterfly likes to live in meadows.

Science spot: your soil

Investigate the natural history of your area. Find out what the soil is like and the different animal and plant species your local area supports. If you have a garden, you could test the soil there.

The square metre project

Ash and Sal have set up a square metre project to find out about the plants and animals that live in the woodland next to their school. They are going to record all the species that grow or visit there.

You will need:

- Four metre-long sticks or lengths of wood
- A record sheet
- Camera

1 Decide where to have your square metre project. Choose an area which has plants and other features that make it a mini habitat.

A mini habitat could contain:
Some pasture
Some meadow
A log
A stone or rock

2 Place the sticks in a square. Take a photograph as a record of how the square looks at the start of the project and photograph the square as it changes during the different seasons.

3 You might decide to divide your square metre into two habitats. You could leave the plants at the back to grow into meadow, and keep the plants at the front shorter like grazed pasture.

4 Visit your square metre regularly and note down all the animals and plants you see there. You might see things like...

Woodlice
Ants
Spiders
Grasshoppers
Beetles
Caterpillars
Snails

5 Try to record and identify each species. Don't forget to turn over stones or look under logs where wildlife may be hiding and to turn them back when finished.

6 Do the same for grasses, wildflowers and berries or leaves you find on your square metre. You can also take close-up photographs as a record and remember to label them with their name and when you saw them.

Here is our record of what we found.

Date: 10th July
Weather: cloudy and dry
Temperature: 22°C

What did we see?

Animals
A woodlouse
A cabbage white butterfly
A grasshopper
Some ants

Plants
Seeding grasses
Purple loosestrife
Broad-leaved dock
Bindweed

What can maps tell us?

Sal and her family are on holiday. Sal has been looking at a map of the area. She has learned what features the different map symbols represent. She has sorted them to show which are new features, which are up to 150 years old and which are even older.

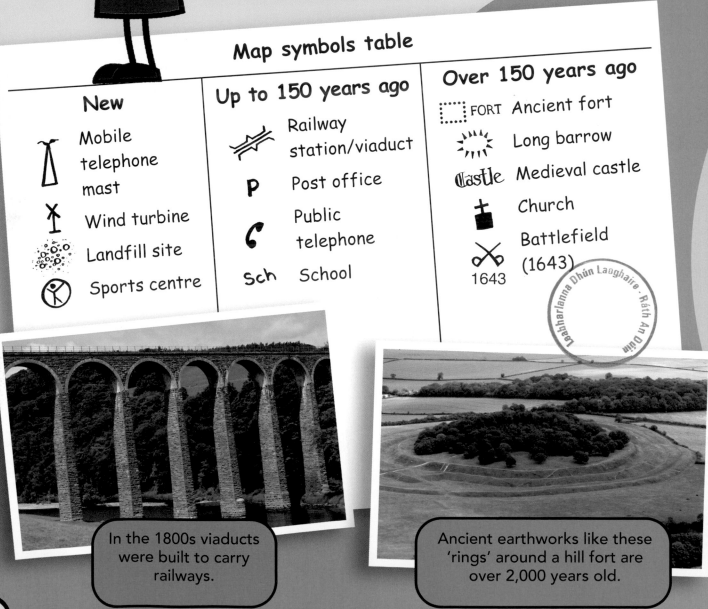

Map symbols table

New	Up to 150 years ago	Over 150 years ago
Mobile telephone mast	Railway station/viaduct	FORT Ancient fort
Wind turbine	P Post office	Long barrow
Landfill site	ℓ Public telephone	Castle Medieval castle
Sports centre	Sch School	† Church
		1643 Battlefield (1643)

In the 1800s viaducts were built to carry railways.

Ancient earthworks like these 'rings' around a hill fort are over 2,000 years old.

Leabharlanna Dhún Laoghaire · Ráth An Dúin

Quiz:

Can you put these features in date order starting with the oldest?

A) A railway

B) A hill fort

C) A telephone mast

Sal reads the contour lines to see whether the land is hilly (where the lines are close together) or flat (where they are wide apart). She uses the map symbols to find marshy land, woodland, parkland and cliffs.

Geography spot: maps of your area

How many of the features on Sal's list can you find on a map of your local area? Can you add more features to each column of the table?

Fast facts: maps

- Street maps show road names and important places and buildings.
- Satellite or aerial maps show major land features like rivers and lakes.
- Road maps show routes of roads, railways tracks and airports.
- Survey maps show hilly or flat land using contours, land features and historical sites.

Make a map stick

Kim and Polly made a map stick when they went to visit a local farm. A map stick tells the story of a walk or journey. Kim and Polly looked around for things to tie on their map stick that would tell the story of their visit.

You will need:

- A bag to collect things you find on your walk
- A stick
- Scissors
- Coloured wool

1 Decide on a place or area where you can go on a walk and find things to make a map stick. It could be a park, woodland or a beach.

2 You need a stick as the base for your map. If there are trees where you are walking, look for a fallen dead stick.

3 Begin to look for things to put on your map stick. They could include leaves, moss, feathers, bark, seeds, sheep's wool and seaweed.

4 When you get home, use the wool to tie the objects you have found to the map stick to tell the story of your journey. You could challenge friends to guess where you have been!

History spot: making records

Map or journey sticks were made by Amerindian peoples to record journeys they had made. In the past, other tribal peoples including the Aboriginal and Maori peoples used songs, dance, spoken stories and drawings as journey records. More recently, travellers have used travel journals and films to record journeys. What other ways can you think of to record journeys you have made?

Changes to your area

Sal is out shopping with her mum and they are visiting a café. Sal's mum tells her the building used to be a bank. When Sal looks at the outside of the building, she can see that it is a grand building with stone carving on the front. She can even see the old bank sign.

STANDARD BANK

Sometimes you can tell how a building was used in the past by looking for signs above the doorway. It may have been a bank, a cinema, a school, a public library or swimming baths. Many old cinemas have been turned into clubs or gyms while some department stores have been divided into several smaller shops.

This music venue was built as a cinema in the 1930s.

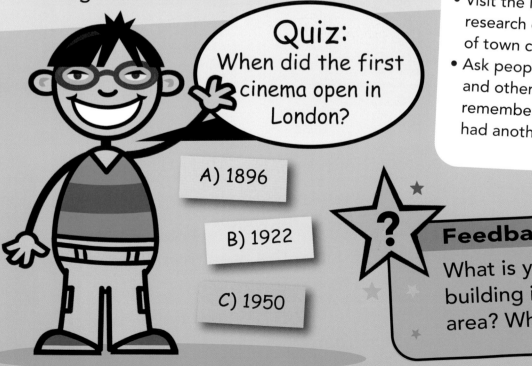

This old town hall building is now being used as a café.

Other buildings such as churches, chapels and barns have been turned into homes for people to live in. Usually you can still see clues to their past, such as Gothic windows in churches or school assembly halls, or the high beamed ceilings of old barns.

Old buildings where you live

- Look for names and signs above doors and windows.
- Look for unusual shaped windows and stained glass in old churches and chapels.
- Visit the local library to research old photographs of town centres.
- Ask people! Grandparents and other relatives may remember when buildings had another use.

Quiz:
When did the first cinema open in London?

A) 1896

B) 1922

C) 1950

?

Feedback...
What is your favourite building in your local area? Why?

Who lives in your area?

Kim has been invited to a Diwali party by his neighbours. Kim knows that Diwali is the Hindu festival of lights. He is taking a gift of sweets for them, and he is looking forward to seeing some fireworks.

Diwali lamps are lit on a Hindu family's shrine.

During the year, there are other festivals in Kim's local area, celebrated by people who have moved there from different parts of the world. Some, like his neighbours, are from India or Pakistan. Others have moved into the area from Eastern Europe to find work. Kim likes to eat at the local Chinese restaurant, and every year the family who run it have special celebrations for Chinese New Year.

Kim knows that his own family have lived in the area since his grandparents moved there, but the community has changed in that time. There is now a Polish church and a mosque where Muslims worship, and there are food stores and restaurants that sell food from all around the world.

Mosques can bring a different style of architecture to an area.

PSHE spot: different cultures

Look for evidence of different cultures and communities living in your area including places of worship, food stores and restaurants.

? Feedback...

Do you live in a multi-cultural area? What do you like about it?

This is Kim's checklist of his local area:

Places of worship
Christian Methodist chapel

Mosque

Polish Roman Catholic church

Food stores
Supermarket

Chinese food store

Polish food store

Restaurants
Chinese restaurant

Indian restaurant

Lebanese restaurant

What jobs do people do?

Sal's class have been finding out about the kinds of job that people do in the local area. First they made a list of all the different resources that could help them.

Advertisements

They looked in the jobs pages of the local newspaper to see what kinds of jobs were advertised. They also found out what jobs were being advertised at the Job Centre. Sal's class collected some job adverts and grouped them under headings that describe the type of employment.

Building and land use

Sal's class also walked around the local area and recorded different ways the land or buildings were used – such as shops, banks, offices, schools, hospitals or garages.

Interviews

Finally, they asked their families and friends what kinds of job they did. They also went into town on market day to carry out a survey asking people where they worked. Everyone in Sal's class added their findings to the class survey. They soon had lots of results! Then they designed a pie chart on the computer to show the percentages of people working for the main employers. What can you tell from the results?

Job Survey Pie Chart
☐ Offices 30%
■ Hotels 19%
☐ Shops 18%
■ Schools 14%
☐ Factories 8%
☐ Hospitals 6%
■ Farming 5%

?

Feedback...

Can you name three main employers of people in your area? What kind of job would you like to do? Could you do that job in your local area?

Make a photo quiz

Kim and Ash are making a photo quiz about their local area. They have been out with their cameras and taken pictures of buildings, objects and features. Polly is helping to cut them out and stick them onto card with quiz questions for people to answer.

You will need:

- Large sheet of card
- Pens and crayons
- Scissors
- Glue
- Camera
- Photographs

1 Take your camera out into your local area and look around for interesting things to photograph. Try to include a variety of buildings, statues and objects.

2 Photograph close-ups or details of things you see – the hand of a statue, a church gargoyle or a post box.

3 Print off the photographs and arrange them on the card. You can use whole photographs or cut out details from them.

4 Next think about the quiz questions you will put in. Make up at least eight. You might have to find out some facts from your local library or the Internet about places you have photographed.

5 Use coloured pens or crayons to write in the quiz questions alongside the photographs, such as:

What is this building used for?

Where would you see this?

Who is this statue of?

Are there problems in your area?

Kim and Polly have been doing a traffic survey on the road that goes past their school. The school is campaigning for a 20 mph zone and a pedestrian crossing to help children cross safely.

They have to prove how busy the road is at peak times when pupils are arriving or leaving, so they are counting all the cars, buses and lorries that go past. First they make a tally chart to count everything. Then they sort all their information into a bar chart.

Vehicle	8.30am — 9.30am	Total	3.30pm — 4.30pm	Total
Lorries	ЖЖ ЖЖ ЖЖ	15	ЖЖ II	7
Buses	ЖЖ ЖЖ ЖЖ ЖЖ II	22	ЖЖ ЖЖ II	12
Bikes	ЖЖ ЖЖ ЖЖ ЖЖ ЖЖ II	27	ЖЖ ЖЖ III	13
Cars	ЖЖ ЖЖ ЖЖ ЖЖ ЖЖ III	28	ЖЖ ЖЖ ЖЖ I	16

Traffic survey tally chart

In a tally chart four lines with a cross across means five items, so there were 27 bikes between 8.30am and 9.30am.

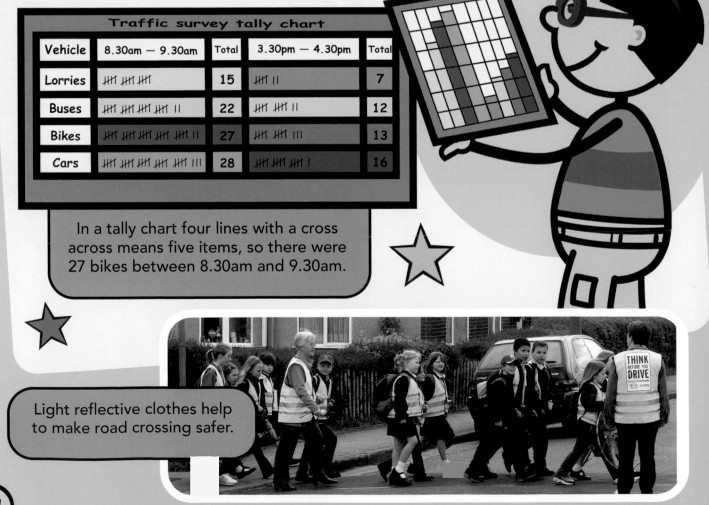

Light reflective clothes help to make road crossing safer.

24

Ash's class have been thinking of other ways that they could improve the area around their school. This is what they wrote on the flipchart.

Hold a litter binge! Clear up all the litter in and around the school grounds.

Clean up graffiti. Get a group of graffiti busters together to clean up the walls in the park.

Plant flowers in hanging baskets and pots for the school grounds.

Graffiti costs time and money to clean up.

PSHE spot: problems in your area

Investigate the problems that affect your local area and ways you could get involved, such as organising a petition or volunteering for a local charity, conservation or wildlife group. There are lots of ways to improve a local area by getting together in groups to take action.

?

Feedback...

Many high streets have empty units where shops have closed down. Can you think of any near you and what the best use might be for them? What amenities are most needed in your community?

Famous connections

Ash has bought some blue glassware for his Gran at a car boot sale. He has learned it is Bristol blue glass so he is reading up about it in a book.

BRISTOL BLUE GLASS

 In the **Middle Ages**, most big towns had a glassmaker.

Bristol grew to be one of the most important glassmaking centres in Europe because of its trading routes across the Atlantic, and a ready supply of coal and materials such as clay and sand.

By the 1780s, Bristol glassmakers had begun to colour the newly-invented lead crystal glass with cobalt oxide to make a rich blue glass. Bristol blue became famous throughout Europe but the industry declined in the 1920s until its revival in 1998.

A Bristol blue goblet.

Local areas can become famous for crafts or food produced there or through connections with famous people or events in history.

Famous Connections

Food
1. Scotland – haggis
2. Derbyshire – Bakewell tart
3. Norfolk – Cromer crabs
4. Wales – laverbread
5. Lancashire hotpot

Crafts
6. Bristol blue glass
7. Arran knitwear
8. Staffordshire pottery

People
9. Stratford-upon-Avon – Shakespeare's birthplace
10. Liverpool – the Beatles

Events
11. Glastonbury, Somerset — annual music festival
12. Notting Hill, London — annual carnival

Sal is making a list of some famous connections for places around Britain.

Geography spot: around Britain

What other famous connections can you think of around Britain?

Quiz:
What colour are tourist attraction signs in the UK?

A) Green

B) Blue

C) Brown

?

Feedback...
Can you name any famous connections that your local area has?

27

Attracting visitors to your area

Sal has been designing a tourist trail for tourists visiting her local area. She has drawn a simple street map and marked interesting things to see and places to visit on the trail.

Tourist Trail

1. Museum
Roman pots and coins. Old farming tools.

2. Viewpoint
Good views over the town from the Old Bridge.

3. Glass factory
See hand-blown glass being made.

4. Arts Centre
Art exhibitions, classes and demonstrations by local craftspeople.

5. Market square
Markets with local produce held Wednesdays and Saturdays.

6. Medieval castle
Walk the ramparts. Visit the dungeons.

Follow me!

Fast facts: tourism – good or bad?

✓ Brings visitors to a local area

✓ Provides jobs in shops, hotels, restaurants, pubs

✓ Brings trade to local businesses and craftspeople

✓ Can bring funding for local amenities

✗ Can endanger land and wildlife if not controlled

✗ Can lead to over-development of countryside

✗ Can cause traffic congestion and other problems to locals

✗ Can be seasonal, i.e. only in summer months

Sal also keeps a scrapbook of tourist attractions around the country that she'd like to visit.

Where I'd like to visit

Historic castles and houses
Edinburgh Castle is famous for the Military Tattoo and a giant cannon called Mons Meg.

Ancient sites and ruins
Stonehenge is Britain's most famous ancient site.

Natural beauty spots
Dorset's coastline attracts fossil hunters looking for ancient fossils in the limestone rocks.

Special events
Wimbledon is famous for its tennis tournament.

Leabharlanna Dhún Laoghaire · Ráth An Dúin

Feedback...

What do you think are the best attractions for tourists in your local area? What tourist attractions would you like to visit?

Glossary

amenities Places that offer services to a community.

barrow Mound of earth or stone that marks a place of burial.

casement Type of window that opens on side hinges.

chapel A type of church.

contour lines Lines on a map that show the height above sea level.

Diwali The Hindu festival of light.

fort A building that is designed to defend people from attack.

gargoyle A carving of a grotesque beast.

gothic A style of architecture dating from the Middle Ages that used pointed arches.

habitat Natural home of living things.

map grid reference Way of finding a location on a map using a grid of lines.

Middle Ages The period from around 1100 to 1600.

mortar Building material used to hold bricks or stones together.

mosque A place of worship for Muslims.

pasture Grassland for grazing animals.

petition A list of signatures requesting something.

species A group of living things that are similar, such as grasses or dogs.

storeys Floors in a building.

traditional Following the customs of the past.

Victorian During the reign of Queen Victoria (1837–1901).

weathervane An arrow or pointer fixed to the top of a building which swings around to show the direction the wind is blowing.

Activity sheets

Go to www.franklinwatts.co.uk/downloads for free worksheets.

Page 6: A checklist like the one Ash used to find out about a building in his local area – it can be used to investigate any building.

Page 26: A map of Britain and space to write in your own ideas for British connections.

Espresso connections

Here are a few ideas for ways you can explore the contents of this book further using Espresso. There are videos you can watch to help you become a history detective, projects you can copy and games you can play. Remember to check the news archives for reports on local heroes and treasures, including artefacts from the past.

What is special about where you live? (pages 4–5)

Watch videos in *Geography 2 > Local study* that show you how you can learn about your local area and how it has changed over time. Investigate the different resources you can use to learn about local heroes and famous events and how to present and interpret your information.

Finding out about the past (pages 6–7)

Find out about the style of buildings in *History 2 > Investigating the past > Tudors times* and *Victorian times* to discover what buildings in your local area can tell you about the past.

What is the natural history of your area? (pages 8–9)

Investigate how one local habitat changes over the seasons in *Science 2 > Habitats > Local habitats* and find out which plants and animals are suited to different habitats. Design your own animal to suit a habitat.

The square metre project (pages 10–11)

Watch videos in *ICT 2 > Data logging* about a school project where the children used a metre of land to grow their own vegetables to eat.

Who lives in your area? (pages 18–19)

Watch videos in *RE 2* about Diwali celebrations, make a Diwali storyboard and look at photos of Diwali customs.

Make a photo quiz (pages 22–23)

Watch videos in *Art 2 > A sense of place* showing a photographer and a landscape artist at work and find out how you can record your own area in photographs and artwork including paint and collage.

Famous connections (pages 26–27)

In *PSHE 2 > Bristol is for me!* Listen to children from different communities living in Bristol, talk about the city and its famous blue glass.

Quiz answers

Page 7: C) Horn
Page 13:
B) A hill fort,
A) A railway,
C) A telephone mast
Page 17: A) 1896
Page 27: C) Brown

These are the lists of contents for each title in *Espresso Ideas Box!*:

Chocolate

Where does chocolate come from? • How do cacao trees grow? • Cacao farming • The history of chocolate • Make a collage of the Aztec chocolate god • The chocolate trade • Make a chocolate piñata • Manufacturing chocolate • Is chocolate good for me? • Melting chocolate • Make chocolate leaves • Chocolate recipes • Chocolate heaven • Glossary and Activity sheets • Espresso connections

Light

Light in the sky • Day and night • The Sun and seasons • Shadow play • Understanding eclipses • Light for life • Seeds and shoots • Rainbows • Make a rainbow spinner • Painting light • Turn the light on! • How do we see? • Holy light • Glossary and Activity sheets • Espresso connections

Rainforests

What is a rainforest? • Rainforests around the world • Rainforest river • Life on the forest floor • Up in the trees • Play the music of the rainforest • Colourful rainforests • Animals in danger • Make a rainforest game • People of the rainorest • Disappearing rainforests • Save the rainforest • Have a rainforest debate • Glossary and Activity sheets • Espresso connections

The Olympics

The Olympic Games • The ancient Olympics • Events at the ancient Olympics • The modern Olympics • Design an Olympic kit • All about the events • Track and field • The Winter Olympics • The Paralympics • Games around the world • What makes an Olympic champion? • Medals and world records • Make an Olympics board game • Glossary and Activity sheets • Espresso connections • Index and quiz answers

Water

Water! • Solid, liquid, gas • The water cycle • Snow, hail and rain • Rivers • Floods • Painting water • Drinking water • Down the drain • Water and plants • Sacred water • Powerful water • Water for fun • Glossary and Activity sheets • Espresso connections

Where you live

What is special about where you live? • Finding out about the past • What is the natural history of your area? • The square metre project • What can maps tell us? • Make a map stick • Changes to your area • Who lives in your area? • What jobs do people do? • Make a picture quiz • What problems are there in your area? • Famous connections • Attracting visitors to your area • Glossary and Activity sheets • Espresso connections